Someone Called Rob

A play in one-act by Martin Lindsay

Moody Lapcat Books

First paperback edition in 2023.

Design and Cover by Martin Lindsay.

Images by Martin Lindsay and Canva.

ISBN: 978-0-6451987-3-7 (paperback)

ISBN: 978-0-6451987-2-0 (ebook)

Published by Moody Lapcat Books

Perth, Western Australia

www.moodylapcatbooks.com

contact@moodylapcatbooks.com

Performing rights

Any performance or public reading of Someone Called Rob is forbidden unless a licence has been received from the author or the author's agent. The purchase of this book in no way gives the purchaser the right to perform the play in public, whether by the means of a staged production or a reading.

All applications for public performance should be directed to the playwright c/- Moody Lapcat Books.

www.moodylapcatbooks.com

contact@moodylapcatbooks.com

Copying for educational purposes

The Australian Copyright Act 1968 (Act) allows a maximum of one chapter or 10% of this book, whichever is the greater, to be reproduced and/or communicated by any educational institution for its educational purposes provided that educational institution or the body that administers it) has given a remuneration notice to Copyright Agency Limited (CAL) under the Act.

For details of the CAL license for educational institutions contact CAL, Level 15, 233 Castlereagh Street, Sydney NSW 2000. Tel: (02) 9394 7600; email: info@copyright.com.au.

Copying for other purposes

Except as permitted under the Act, for example a fair dealing for the purposes of study, research, criticism or review, all rights are reserved. This publication (or any part of it) may

Characters

ROB – 20s/30s

"I've watched The Godfather. Nothing good ever comes of this sort of thing."

An easy-going bachelor, until a silly simple flirtation sends his life into anxiety and paranoia.

ADAM – 20s/30s

"You do and I will <u>crush</u> you, mate."

An aggressive no-nonsense brute with a major jealous streak.

KATE – 20s/30s

"Maybe next time, you'll think before signing a complete stranger's birthday card. No matter how hot they may be."

A vain princess whose tastes in men change as frequently as her nail polish.

JACINTA – 20s/30s

"Is this that creepy bloke from the pub? I told you to piss off."

Kate's very opinionated, very outspoken, and often very angry best mate.

The cast playing Adam, Kate and Jacinta also play:

- POWER COMPANY INSPECTOR (M/F)

- OLD LADY neighbour (F)

- TELEMARKETER (M/F)

- FEMALE VOICE IN THROES OF PASSION (F)

- IT SUPPORT (M/F)

- BARMAID (F)

- DRUNK BLOKE (M)

- TAMMY, Jacinta's Drunk friend (F)

- FRIEND OF A MATE'S EX (F)

Setting

The stage is divided into two areas, allowing fast transitions and simultaneous scenes.

On one side is ROB'S FLAT, a twenty-something guy's apartment containing:

- COUCH and COFFEE TABLE

- DESK with chair and "LAPTOP".

- A DOORMAT marking an invisible "FRONT DOOR".

- Proscenium or side of stage is Rob's shadowy "PORCH" and "GARDEN".

- An electricity METER BOX is mounted on the proscenium/side wall.

On the other side is ELSEWHERE, a bare space that doubles as other houses, Rob's garage, a bar, etc.

The two settings are divided by a narrow bench or counter, at an angle.

- From ROB'S FLAT side, it acts as his "KITCHEN" counter.

- From "ELSEWHERE", it can be used as Rob's "CAR", a pub "BAR", etc.

NOTE: "" indicates imaginary/mimed prop or location.

Production Notes

ROB's FLAT and ELSEWHERE should have independent lighting, in order to fade areas in and out as required.

If back projection is possible, the following pictures/graphics are to be displayed:

- A decapitated mouse's head upon a doormat.
- A close-up of a reasonably angry duck.

A gauze/scrim frame at the rear of ROB'S FLAT lit to allow ADAM's silhouette to briefly appear and disappear. Alternatively, this could be achieved by shadow or back projection.

Props and locations enclosed in double-quotes are imaginary, and are either mimed, or indicate specific off-stage areas.

First Performed

Melville Theatre Company, February 2013.

Directed by Jeff Hansen.

Original Cast

- Rob – Rob Gander
- Adam and others – Faraz Hedayat
- Kate and others – Ruhama Geiger
- Jacinta and others – Annie Blatchford

Dedicated to the memory of Jeff Hansen.

You would have been relieved to know I've slightly cut down the number of lighting cues.

Someone Called Rob

SOUND FX: Rob's Mobile ringtone.

LIGHTS UP "ROB'S FLAT".

ROB enters sleepily, wearing clothes from the previous night.

ROB picks up MOBILE and squints at screen.

NOTE: Rob alternates between speaking directly to audience and interacting in the present moment, indicated in bracket directions.

ROB

(Audience) I usually let unknown numbers through to voicemail. You know ... telemarketers.

ROB answers MOBILE.

LIGHTS UP "ELSEWHERE".

ADAM is an angry young man on a MOBILE.

ADAM

Is that Rob?

ROB

(Audience) He sounded ready to explode.
A hangover made my "Who wants to know?" a
bit gruffer than I intended.

ADAM

I'm the boyfriend of Kate.

ROB

(Audience) The call now involved two strangers. I asked who Kate was in order to narrow things down.

ADAM

Kate is the girl whose birthday card you signed at the pub last night.

ROB

Oh.

ROB casts his bleary mind back.

SOUND FX: Muffled bar sounds.

ROB

(Audience) Vague recollection….
I *did* sign something. My mate's card? But it wasn't his birthday.

ROB shakes his head – a bad idea, given his hangover.

SOUND FX: Muffled bar sounds fade.

ROB

(Phone) Are you sure?

2

ADAM

You left this phone number on the card, too.

ROB

(Audience) More recollection ... *(Dread)* Oh god.

SOUND FX: Bar sounds – drinks clinking, chat and shouts.

ROB

Late in the night. A few too many beers.
When every fleeting idea suddenly seems an
unbackable winner.

LIGHTS – Mood lighting in "ROB's FLAT".

ADAM freezes as ...

LIGHTS DOWN "ELSEWHERE"

ROB

There was a chance Kate had been *gorgeous.*
There was equal chance the beers were talking.
This Adam guy seemed quite taken with her, so
obviously gorgeous enough for me to gate-crash
her birthday gathering at the pub. Then cheekily
sign her card with a flirtatious witticism and – oh
crap – my mobile number.
The witticism was less a romantic sonnet, more a
mildly pornographic pick-up line.

SOUND quickly fades.

LIGHTS back UP in "ROB's FLAT" and "ELSEWHERE"

ADAM returns to life.

ADAM

What are you playing at, making a pass at my
girlfriend?

ROB

(Audience) That would probably explain the anger.
I babbled an apology – me drunk, the hour late,
the beers many.
(Phone) And most definitely not aware that you
were on the scene in a romantic sense or
otherwise.

ADAM

Otherwise?

ROB

(Phone) Otherwise, I wouldn't have done it.

ADAM wavers, unconvinced.

ADAM

Well, it better not happen again.

ROB

(Audience) I barely remembered it happening in
the first place. He hung up with a parting cuss.

ADAM mouths something derogatory.

4

LIGHTS DOWN "ELSEWHERE".

ROB

I made a new resolution, effective immediately.
No more tequila slammers when random birthday
cards were around.

*ROB puts MOBILE in back pocket only to find the remains of a
KEBAB. ROB sniffs KEBAB then shrugs.*

ROB

Breakfast is served.

*ROB flops onto COUCH, puts MOBILE aside to unwrap KEBAB
and take a bite when …*

SOUND FX: Rob's Mobile ringtone.

ROB

Another unknown number.

ROB answers MOBILE warily.

ROB

Hello?

LIGHTS UP "ELSEWHERE".

KATE stands annoyed, hand on hip, on MOBILE.

KATE

Is that someone called Rob?

5

ROB

(Audience) I confirmed with less courage this time.

KATE

This is Kate. You wrote *something* in my birthday card last night.

ROB

(Phone) Ah. Sorry about that. In fact, your boyfriend just rang to point out the error of my … harmless prank.

KATE is immediately worried.

KATE

Adam called you? Shit, I didn't think he'd seen it. What did he say? He didn't *threaten* you, did he?

ROB

(Audience, worried) Threaten?
(Phone) Threaten?

KATE

Violently. Physically. Christ, you didn't give him your address, did you?

ROB

(Audience) My mind replayed the previous conversation at high speed. *(Thinks)* No. I'd barely even confirmed my name. Safe! Reasonably. *(Phone)* No threats. Just some perfectly understandable anger in the circumstances.

KATE

You don't know Adam.

ROB

(Audience) This was true. Or her for that matter.
I told Kate I'd explained everything to Adam. She
thanked me for being so understanding.

KATE

Thanks for being so understanding. And maybe
next time, you'll think before signing a complete
stranger's birthday card. *(Checks fingernails)* No
matter how hot they may be.

ROB

(Audience) I apologised again, though mentioning
how if she didn't have a boyfriend, this call
might've turned out better. She laughed politely.

KATE

(Barely polite unamused laugh) Ha.

ROB

(Audience) It probably wasn't the time for flirting.

Unimpressed, KATE hangs up then departs OFF.

LIGHTS DOWN "ELSEWHERE".

ROB

Then, barely twenty minutes later …

SOUND FX: Rob's Mobile ringtone

ROB warily answers MOBILE.

LIGHTS UP "ELSEWHERE".

An even angrier ADAM is on MOBILE.

ADAM

I *cannot* believe you.

ROB

(Phone) Adam?

ADAM

I tell you off for cracking on to Kate, then next thing, you're secretly calling her behind my back.

ROB

It wasn't a secret call.

ADAM

It was secret from me.

ROB

It was secret from me that it was secret. So, technically it was only half-secret. *(Confused)* Or would that be double secret?

ADAM

You are treading on dangerously thin ice, mate.

ROB

I didn't call behind your back! She did.

ADAM

So, you admit it!

ROB

How was I to know she does things behind your back?

ADAM

(Suspicious) What's she doing behind my back?

ROB

Just calling me, as far as I know.

ADAM

Right, I'm gonna bloody do you, mate!

ROB

She just rang to clear things up. How did you find out anyway?

ADAM

I checked her phone.

ROB

Behind her back?

ADAM

I can hardly go through it in front of her.

ROB

Then you'll see from her call history that she has only ever called me *once*. Just then. So, there isn't anything going on. Not with me anyway.

ADAM

Are you saying there's something going on with someone else?

ROB

No. Yes. Maybe. I don't know. How would I know what she gets up to?

ADAM

She's getting up to something?

ROB

I don't know!

ADAM

Why are you saying this stuff about Kate? You trying to cover up what you're really up to with her?

ROB

I'm not saying anything about Kate! She didn't say the call was secret or full of coded messages.

ADAM

Well, what did you think, her calling you out of the blue?

ROB

I didn't think anything. I don't calculate the secrecy potential of calls from numbers I don't know before answering them.
(Audience) Though from now on, I definitely will!

ADAM

Mr Fancy clever talker, eh?

ROB

(Phone) A clever guy would've hung up by now.

ADAM

You do and I will *crush* you, mate.

ROB takes a calming breath.

ROB

(Audience) Fortunately, diplomacy ran in my family. I invoked the universal signal of utmost honesty between guys.
(Phone) Dude. I don't have designs on your girlfriend. You're a lucky man, and I wish you all the best with her. Nothing's going on.

ADAM considers this, wavering.

ROB

(Audience) Silence on the line. The 'Dude' had done its work.

ADAM

There better not be, eh. Because if I find out

you're calling each other again …

ROB

(Phone) I don't even know her number.
(Audience) Or I wouldn't after completely clearing
my phone history the moment this call was over.
(Phone) Good as forgotten. Like it never
happened.

ADAM

(Suspicious) You said it didn't happen.

ROB

It didn't.

ADAM

It better not have.

ROB

I wish.

ADAM, still unsatisfied, hangs up.

LIGHTS DOWN "ELSEWHERE".

ROB

(Audience) There was a conversation about to be
had, and I was glad to have no further part in it.

*ROB places MOBILE on COFFEE TABLE then opens "FRONT
DOOR". He steps out yawning and scratching himself.*

ROB

Other than that, it seemed a nice morning. *(Looks up to bright "SUN")* … Afternoon.

ROB yawns his way back inside, glances at MOBILE in passing. He snatches it up in surprise.

ROB

Kate had rung back three times. I didn't dare listen to the voicemails.

ROB presses at MOBILE, selecting options.

ROB

I immediately blocked her number and cleared my voicemail. No more answering unknown callers for me!

ROB adamantly places MOBILE down, then moves to "KITCHEN" and dries dishes with TEA TOWEL, humming to himself.

SOUND FX: Rob's MOBILE ring tone.

ROB's humming deflates. He warily checks MOBILE.

ROB

A completely different number I didn't recognise called on Sunday evening.

He determinedly places MOBILE down.

ROB

No. *(Watches the MOBILE with growing unease)*
Curiosity versus better judgement.

He steps forward to almost pick up MOBILE.

ROB

Curiosity. *(He steps back)* Better judgement.

He picks up MOBILE.

ROB

(Audience) So kill me.

LIGHTS UP "ELSEWHERE".

An angry young woman, JACINTA is on a MOBILE.

JACINTA

Who *the frick* do you think you are?

ROB

(Phone) I don't know. Who do you think I am?

JACINTA

Some thoughtless bastard stirring up trouble for a
laugh. Surely you know how rocky things are
between Adam and Kate?

ROB

(Audience) I groaned at the names, then asked
hers.

14

JACINTA

I'm Jacinta. Kate's best friend, who looks out for her when pricks like you come along, screwing her around.

ROB

(*Audience*) My protests of innocence were ignored.

JACINTA

Adam is furious! He's talking about ending it all.

ROB

(*Phone*) What, suicide?

JACINTA

No, with Kate. He totally doesn't trust her anymore, with you leaving messages and suggesting things.

ROB

I haven't suggested anything.

JACINTA

That's not what Kate says.

ROB

I don't even know Kate. She's been ringing me.

JACINTA

Don't blame this on her, you shit.

ROB

I'm not!

JACINTA

Just as well, arsehole. Things are still tense between them about the whole Scott thing.

ROB

Who's Scott?

JACINTA

Don't try acting stupid.

ROB

I'm not acting.

JACINTA

Scott was the guy Adam thought Kate was seeing behind his back. And *we all know* what happened between Adam and Scott.

ROB

I don't.

JACINTA

Well, you wouldn't want it to happen to you.

ROB

(Audience) This is exactly what you don't want to hear in the information age. In fact, this information was aging me at a fast rate.

LIGHTS in "ROB'S FLAT" grow slowly sinister.

ROB

I had visions of Adam as some ogre of a guy

googling me down.

*ADAM enters with CHAIR and sits at FRONT of
"ELSEWHERE" as though staring at a "SCREEN".*

*As ROB monologues, ADAM periodically pounds a "KEYBOARD"
like a caveman with occasional precise "MOUSE" adjustments.*

ROB

A mobile number and a first name – that's all you
need these days to trace someone. There's
probably enough casual information online to
clean out my bank account, let alone trace my
home address.

ADAM delights at some discovery on "SCREEN".

ROB

For all I knew, he'd find a picture of my house
online, for all to see and stake out. The internet is
a stalker's paradise.

ADAM types at "KEYBOARD" with glee.

ROB

He could post it to his mates! Doxxing it's called.
Releasing your victim's details to your own
personal social media lynch-mob. Dog-whistling
them into action to make someone's life a misery.

ROB rushes to "WINDOW", looking out.

17

ADAM *stands ominously, then circles back to sneak into the rear of* "ROB's FLAT" *as ROB speaks, lurking a distance behind ROB.*

ROB

He could sneak round at any time. Break in at any moment. Waiting till I'm at my most helpless and vulnerable to make his move.

ROB *begins "washing" as though in the shower, scrubbing with* MOBILE *like soap.*

ADAM *slowly moves in towards ROB.*

ROB

I could be in the shower. Slowly, he moves in, grabbing the nearest weapon to hand. Then when I least expect, he attacks! Stabbing me with a bottle of Toilet Duck!

SOUND FX: *"Psycho" music – four intense violin strikes.*

ADAM *stabs at ROB with imaginary* "TOILET DUCK BOTTLE" *in time to the music strikes.*

FX: *Backdrop flashes picture of an angry duck with each strike.*

ROB *cinematically falls to his knees, as though knifed in the back.*

ADAM *quickly prowls OFF.*

LIGHTS UP "ELSEWHERE".

JACINTA

It would serve you right if it did.

LIGHTS in "ROB'S FLAT" back to normal.

ROB comes to, realising he's still in phone conversation.

ROB

(Phone) Why does Adam jump to these sorts of
conclusions?
(Audience) There was a scoffing sound at the other
end of the line.

JACINTA

(Haughty scoffing sound)

ROB recoils from MOBILE.

ROB

(Audience) She was either disgusted by the
question or coughing up something nasty.
(Phone) Why did Adam think Scott and Kate were
seeing each other?

JACINTA

Because they were. God, everyone knew that.

ROB

Except Adam presumably. To begin with, anyway.

JACINTA

This isn't a laughing matter.

ROB peers nervously out "WINDOW".

ROB

I'm not laughing.

JACINTA

Adam's severely pissed off. Just like with Scott. *(Ominous)* And we *all* know what happened to Scott.

ROB

What happened to Scott?

JACINTA

What *didn't* happen to Scott.

ROB swallows hard at the unspoken implications.

ROB

(Audience) Was my door locked?

ROB checks "FRONT DOOR" – locked!

ROB

(Phone, desperate) Look, my intentions in all this were entirely honourable.
(Audience) I was giving my inebriated self significant benefit of the doubt.
(Phone) I didn't even have any intentions. It was just a drunken joke.

JACINTA

Oh, charming!

ROB

(Phone, slow and deliberate) I thought Kate was single. I've since discovered she isn't, so I've backed away. Well away. Over the hill and far far away. I thought I'd explained all that to Adam. So hopefully this is the last he, she, you and especially me hear any more of this.

JACINTA

Dick.

JACINTA angrily hangs up and stomps OFF.

LIGHTS DOWN "ELSEWHERE".

ROB

(Audience) It took me a moment to work out who Dick was. *(Reacts, insulted)* I was definitely changing my number *first thing in the morning.*

LIGHTS UP "ELSEWHERE".

KATE furiously messages on MOBILE, sitting in the CHAIR. JACINTA nods encouragement over her shoulder.

KATE

A drunken joke am I!

SOUND FX: Message on ROB's Mobile.

KATE and JACINTA stomp OFF, taking CHAIR with them.

LIGHTS DOWN "ELSEWHERE".

ROB looks at MOBILE, flinches.

ROB

I was definitely changing my number *straight away.*

ROB sits at DESK, types at "KEYBOARD".

ROB

To be sure, I opted for a new random number. It was a hassle – I'd have to change a lot of details – but enough was definitely enough.

ROB taps "Enter" triumphantly.

ROB

It would take a few hours to take effect.

Satisfied, ROB switches off MOBILE and lays it on DESK.

ROB

Off, away and out of mind.

ROB eyes MOBILE, taps his knees impatiently. He quickly removes BACK COVER from MOBILE.

ROB

I took out the battery just in case.

ROB stands decisively.

ROB

Besides, a whole evening away from the phone –
Paradise! We're like addicts, constantly checking
calls and messages, updating our statuses. We
should switch off like this more often. There's
more to life than technology!

*ROB is immediately restless. He checks his wrist – no watch. He gazes
forlornly at MOBILE, then turns away.*

*Cold turkey hits – ROB clutches himself, itchy and uncomfortable. He
gazes longingly to MOBILE.*

Decisively, ROB sits at DESK, determined.

ROB

Maybe a look on the internet instead.

ROB types at "KEYBOARD", investigating a hunch.

ROB

I searched for myself online. Luckily, I'd long ago
given up on social media. I'd deactivated all my
various face-toks, and hangarounds and insta-
twats. But can you ever *really* deactivate? *You*
might call it quits, but *they* don't give your
information up without a fight. Their honey traps
lure us in, never to ever really escape. All those
things innocently posted, naively in the moment,
forevermore to haunt us. Or hunt us down with.

ROB is appalled by results on "SCREEN".

23

ROB

Oh god, how did *that* photo get online?

ROB clicks "MOUSE" in increasing horror.

ROB

How did *all* of this get there?

ROB checks his wrist – again, no watch – then checks "SCREEN".

ROB

Midnight already?

ROB stands then warily picks up MOBILE.

ROB

Surely it was safe by now.

ROB replaces COVER on MOBILE, switches on. Relief! He holds MOBILE to chest lovingly.

ROB

A new phone number. A new life of freedom.

ROB presses at MOBILE as he talks.

ROB

I deleted all remaining trace of them. Contacts.
Call history. Messages. Everything. ... All gone.

ROB sets MOBILE on DESK in triumph.

ROB

I was now rid of Adam, Kate, Jacinta, Scott, and whoever else in their bizarre little love-triangle world forever! *(Sighs contentedly)* I would sleep well tonight!

ROB departs to "BEDROOM", stopping at "LIGHT SWITCH".

ROB

(Audience) Night night.

ROB flicks "LIGHT SWITCH".

LIGHTS DOWN ROB'S FLAT.

ROB departs OFF.

SOUND FX: Dog barking.

ROB rushes back ON, looks about, then departs OFF again in relief.

LIGHT EFFECT: ADAM's silhouette lurks.

LIGHT EFFECT slow FADE OUT.

SOUND FX: Greig's "Peer Gynt"

LIGHTS FADE UP in ROB's FLAT.

SOUND FX: Rob's Mobile bleeps an SMS.

25

ROB stomps ON in T-SHIRT and BOXERS.

ROB

What sort of psycho mental case messages at 7 in the morning? *(Halts, full of doubt)* Maybe the psycho mental case out there trying to get me?

ROB hesitantly checks MOBILE.

ROB

A phone company customer feedback survey for their online number transfer services. *(Sarcastic)* Oh yes, absolutely overjoyed.

ROB sets MOBILE down then plods to "WINDOWS".

ROB

Might as well enjoy the early start.

ROB opens "CURTAINS" wide, blinks from daylight, then immediately alarmed.

ROB

A strange car sat in my driveway.

ROB immediately closes "CURTAINS".

ROB

Had I been seen?

ROB opens "CURTAINS" to quickly peer out, then immediately pulls them together again. He's pulled too hard! ROB reaches to pull the outer

*sides of the "CURTAINS" outwards. Now a gap in the centre reveals
him! With a yelp, ROB pulls "CURTAINS" together again then
scurries to hide behind DESK.*

ROB

How long had it been there? In *my* driveway, my
territory. A hunter – a *predator* – ready to attack at
will. I armed myself!

ROB grabs nearby SPATULA then looks to "FRONT DOOR".

ROB

No knock, no doorbell. No forced entry … yet.
Had I been seen? Or was he just toying?

ROB "tick tocks" the SPATULA from side to side.

ROB

Minutes passed.

ROB sneaks to "WINDOW" to peer out "CURTAINS".

ROB

The car was definitely lurking. Watching the
house, waiting. It could only be Adam.

ROB backs from "WINDOW", agitated.

ROB

Could I escape? If I wasn't safe in my own home,
where could I be?

ROB grips SPATULA firmly as a weapon.

ROB

I *could* walk out and confront him. I *should* walk
out and confront him. Like a man, not a mouse.

SPATULA droops in ROB's hand.

ROB

Or just sit it out. Like a manly mouse. He'd see
sense eventually. We're both rational human
beings. Well, I was.

Still holding SPATULA aloft, ROB peers out "CURTAINS".

ROB

Five minutes or five hours? Still, he waited.
Until…

Movement catches ROB's eye.

ROB

My neighbour dashed out with a tennis racquet
and hopped in the passenger seat.

SOUND FX: Car driving off.

ROB watches "CAR" depart then turns to SPATULA in relief

ROB

False alarm.

Aware he's talking to it, ROB hides SPATULA behind back.

ROB

Some might call me paranoid.

VOICES

(Off) You're paranoid!

ROB looks about, realises no one is there.

ROB

And well you might. But I do have precedent.
Way back, I was bullied by the bigger kid who
lived down my street.

*ADAM wearing BICYCLE HELMET "cycles" in on "BIKE"
behind ROB. He pulls up in a skid. shaking a fist and pulling fingers,
mouthing insults, and throwing "rocks".*

ROB

Every time I went out to play, he'd cycle up to
threaten me, or call me names, or throw sticks
and stones. *(Cowers)* Months I spent, too scared to
go out and play. But I was safe. Locked away
where he couldn't get me.
Turned out he'd moved house weeks earlier.

*ADAM is "called home" from off-stage then sulkily "rides" OFF,
flipping a last two-fingers at ROB.*

ROB

Maybe it made me just that bit more timid and
wary. The kid who's always too scared to jump in

29

the deep end of the swimming pool.

ROB looks over "edge" of "SWIMMING POOL", wary of dangers.

ROB

Always worried about what might be down there,
waiting to get you.

ADAM enters and cheerfully pushes ROB "in" who yelps in surprise.

ROB

Only for the bullies of this world to push you in.
Just for a laugh.

ADAM chortles, then departs OFF with a last flipping of two-fingers.

ROB

(Determined) You can't take any chances with these
psychos. It's defend yourself or perish.

*ROB brandishes SPATULA, realises what he's holding, then tosses it
aside. He steps forward and peers out "CURTAINS" again.*

ROB

Maybe, like years ago, Adam might simply move
on if I just stay locked down, inside. Hiding.

Relief! It's all clear.

*ROB decisively draws "CURTAINS" open wide. He returns to
COUCH and opens MAGAZINE as distraction.*

ROB casually glances at "WINDOW".

ROB

Another car pulled into my drive not long after. I wasn't falling for that again! *(Continues reading)* It idled, engine running.

ROB peers over MAGAZINE.

ROB

Still there.

ROB concentrates on MAGAZINE, but glances to "WINDOW".

ROB

Still there.

ROB decisively holds MAGAZINE in front of face. He peers around MAGAZINE.

ROB

This was different. This car was actively *lurking* with intent.

ROB approaches "WINDOW", tension building and peers out.

ROB

The sun visor obscured the driver's face. But he was sitting, staring, straight at my window. At me. Adam? Had he found me? *(Watches in horror)* The driver was mouthing words. Curses. Threats of violence he was about to inflict?

31

ROB squints, lip-reading. He translates aloud slowly.

ROB

I will crush you.
I will destroy you.
See you next Tuesday.
Okey dokes bye bye.

ROB recoils from "WINDOW".

ROB

The driver reached forward – for a knife? A gun?
A candlestick? Lead piping? *(Frowns)* Or just
hanging up a phone call on his hands-free mobile
that he pulled off the road to take.

ROB waves weakly back to "DRIVER" as "CAR" departs.

SOUND FX: Car driving off.

ROB looks to Audience guiltily.

ROB

Some *would* call it paranoia.

ROB expects the voices – none are forthcoming. He glances at Audience in concern, then paces in agitation.

ROB

I'm rational enough to recognise my imagination
might be running away with silly, unrelated events.
But they kept happening. Noises in the night.

SOUND FX: A crash then a cat shriek.

ROB looks up to ceiling.

SOUND FX: Voices arguing.

ROB
Shouting in the street.

ROB rushes to look out "WINDOW".

SOUND FX: Tapping on glass

ROB
The tree that tapped spookily on the kitchen window, randomly tapping my window spookily. But was it just the tree?

SOUND FX: Rhythmic thumping of bedhead on wall.

ROB points to side "WALL".

ROB
(Audience) Was *this* just in my imagination?

FEMALE VOICE IN THROES OF PASSION
Yes!

ROB
No.

FEMALE VOICE IN THROES OF PASSION
Yes!

ROB
No.

FEMALE VOICE IN THROES OF PASSION
Oh yes!

ROB looks to side of stage.

SOUND FX: Rhythmic thumping gives a last few quick then weaker thumps before finally stopping.

ROB / FEMALE VOICE IN THROES OF PASSION
(ROB in realisation, HER in relief) Ohhhhh.

ROB
Okay, maybe just the thin walls to my neighbour's bedroom. But there were other things, like the next morning ...

SOUND FX: Rob's MOBILE ring tone.

ROB yawns then blearily answers MOBILE, rubbing his eyes.

SOUND FX: Angry gabble on phone line.

ROB holds MOBILE from ear, a tirade coming down the line.

ROB

My boss, angrily asking if I was gracing work
with my presence today. Work?

Alarmed, ROB checks his wrist — no watch — then MOBILE.

ROB

Holy crap!

ROB races OFF to "BEDROOM" …

*… quickly reappearing with TIE loosely around neck, one arm in
JACKET, and frantically brushing teeth with TOOTHBRUSH.*

ROB throws TOOTHBRUSH aside and dons JACKET.

ROB

(Mouthful of "toothpaste") My alarm clock - …

*ROB spits "TOOTHPASTE" into hand. What to do with it? ROB
shoves hand in pocket, wincing.*

ROB

My alarm clock was dead to the world. There
must have been a power failure overnight!

*ROB almost strangles himself pulling up TIE, then races out
"FRONT DOOR". He stops, looking at POWER BOX on wall.*

ROB

Or a power *cut?* No. Blackouts happen all the
time. *(Suspicious)* But it didn't hurt to check.

ROB treads carefully through "GARDEN", opens POWER BOX.

ROB

My mains circuit breaker had tripped during the night. Odd. *Or* had it been deliberately switched? (Points) The meter box just sitting on the front wall. For anyone to waltz up and tamper with.

ROB scours the ground.

ROB

Footprints in the garden bed? ...Nothing.

ROB raises foot, having stepped in something nasty.

ROB

Except for discovering where my cat did her business.

ROB takes "PADLOCK" from pocket, attaches to POWER BOX.

ROB

That evening, I attached a padlock to the meter box. Ha!

Reassured, ROB unlocks "FRONT DOOR" as ...

INSPECTOR in HIGH-VIS VEST and HARDHAT with CLIPBOARD arrives to find POWER BOX "padlocked".

INSPECTOR

Oi!

ROB turns round. INSPECTOR sternly points to POWER BOX.

ROB

(Audience) Until told to remove it when a power company guy inspected my meter.

INSPECTOR

Yeeeeah, nah mate.

ROB quickly removes "PADLOCK".

They both react to a bad smell, look around sniffing. They check their shoes then wipe them on ground.

ROB

Bloody cat.

INSPECTOR waggles a reprimanding finger then departs.

ROB

My power box became a sitting duck once more. Leaving *me* a sitting duck for any stray act of tampering or malicious intent.

ROB walks to centre-stage "LETTERBOX" as OLD LADY neighbour totters ON from right.

ROB checks for mail – nothing.

ROB

(Audience) No mail again?

OLD LADY hands over LETTERS.

ROB

Again?

OLD LADY nods.

ROB

(Audience) Mail kept "accidentally" arriving in the wrong mailbox.

OLD LADY is unable to see who he is talking to.

ROB

Too many times for us to just cheerfully joke about our dopey postman.

ROB and OLD LADY mime gentle laughter. ROB stops, but OLD LADY continues laughing heartily. And laughing.

ROB

(Audience) She doesn't get out much.

ROB waves goodbye but OLD LADY grips her nose and points at his shoes.

ROB checks shoes, then wipes them on the ground.

ROB

Bloody cat.

OLD LADY totters OFF.

ROB

Sometimes, my phone would ring -

SOUND FX: Rob's Mobile rings, until …

ROB rushes round to enter through "FRONT DOOR".

SOUND FX … stops just as ROB reaches MOBILE.

ROB

Only to stop just before I could answer.

ROB checks MOBILE.

ROB

Private number. No message.

ROB places MOBILE down then regards it with suspicion.

ROB

Sometimes just one ring.

SOUND FX: ROB Mobile – one quick ring/bleep.

ROB reaches for MOBILE, but it has stopped.

ROB

Sometimes just a few.

ROB crouches over MOBILE, ready to snatch it up.

Nothing. He stands, disappointed.

ROB

Totally unpredictable.

SOUND FX: ROB Mobile – one quick ring/bleep.

ROB glares at MOBILE, tosses LETTERS onto COFFEE TABLE then walks out "FRONT DOOR" and across to "ELSEWHERE".

ROB

Maybe they were all telemarketers, wrong numbers, and Nigerian Princes overstocked with Viagra. "So, don't answer" you say. The trouble was, I already had in the first place.

LIGHTS UP "ELSEWHERE".

ROB notices "front wheel" of his "CAR".

ROB

Then I found a flat tyre on my car.

Groaning, ROB opens "BOOT" of "CAR".

ROB

The spare was flat too. Though that was more my general neglect.

SOUND FX: ROB's MOBILE rings only once.

ROB glares back at "HOUSE" then bends down to examine "TYRE" of "CAR".

ROB

I checked for sabotage. Adam didn't seem the psychological terrorist type. But psychological terrorists never do. Who knew what the insanely jealous were capable of? And what *had* Adam done to Steve? Simon? Scott? *(Shrugs)* That other guy.

ROB quickly checks underneath "CAR".

ROB

No bombs.

Noticing something, ROB withdraws "SCREW" from "TYRE".

ROB

A screw. Embedded in the tyre grooves. *(Trying to remain calm)* It was entirely possible a screw might lay on the road. And that I might happen to drive over it. Totally possible it punctured the *exact* weak spot of my tyre tread.

ROB backs from "CAR", slowly returns to "FRONT DOOR".

ROB

Was it *all* just bad luck and coincidence?

ROB stops short before DOORMAT.

ROB

And then I found the mouse head.

FX: "MOUSEHEAD ON DOORMAT" PICTURE ON BACK WALL

SOUND FX: OMINOUS BLARING CHORD

ROB

(Slow, dreaded) Just a head. In the middle of my doormat. Waiting. Its cold dead eyes stared untold menace. It was a message: "This will be you". I've watched The Godfather. Nothing good ever comes of this sort of thing.

FX: "MOUSEHEAD ON DOORMAT" FADES OUT.

ROB

Yes, it could have been my cat, leaving food for her starving master. Exactly dead centre on the doormat. *(Looks again)* Was it just my imagination that the entrails spelt out "You Next"?

SOUND FX: ROB's Mobile rings, ongoing.

ROB rushes through "FRONT DOOR", snatches up MOBILE.

ROB

I demanded the caller identify themself!

LIGHTS UP "ELSEWHERE".

A cheery, dubiously accented TELEMARKETER *stands wearing* HEADSET.

TELEMARKETER

Hello there and goo-day mate.

ROB

Oh God.

TELEMARKETER

I am the wondering if you would be considering the automatic roller door for your garage?

ROB

No.

TELEMARKETER

It would be very nice.

ROB

Would it be *lockable*?

TELEMARKETER

For you, I will do the checking.

TELEMARKETER types on "KEYBOARD".

TELEMARKETER

Only in blue. No ochre.

ROB

What? No, I said *lockable*, not ochre. Is it secure?

43

TELEMARKETER

Payment is very secure, sir. In the four very easy instalments.

ROB

I'm not interested.

TELEMARKETER

Okay! Two easy instalments, followed by two even easier instalments.

ROB

No thank you.

TELEMARKETER

All doors come with the deadbolt locking facility. Would that be interesting to sir?

ROB

Only if it can keep out psychotically jealous boyfriends.

TELEMARKETER

Oh! You are having the boyfriend troubles?

ROB

Am I ever!

TELEMARKETER

Take my advice. Take him for the nice night out then give him the foot rub when you get home. Ooh-la-la!

LIGHTS DOWN "ELSEWHERE".

ROB hangs up then paces methodically.

ROB

A mobile number and a first name. From a name
to an address. From there, a letterbox. Inside:
identifying information. Medical details, account
numbers. Email is no safer. We casually give out
our identity. Sign up here. PINs and passwords
remembered. Credit cards saved "for your
convenience".

ROB stops in fear.

ROB

How easy for Adam to sign me into something
dodgy then tell the police?

ROB looks to "ELSEWHERE".

ROB

Had the neighbours seen anyone at my letterbox?

LIGHTS UP "ELSEWHERE".

OLD LADY neighbour stands, thinking, then shakes head.

ROB glares accusingly.

ROB

Had any neighbours been blabbing anything and

45

everything about me to complete strangers?

OLD LADY holds up hand in oath, crosses heart, shakes head.

ROB

Are you *sure?*

OLD LADY bows head, shuffles feet guiltily.

ROB scurries to "WALL", places ear to listen.

OLD LADY begins talking animatedly.

ROB

(Listening at wall) The old lady next door was notorious for knowing far too much about our street. And only too keen to broadcast the spiciest titbits. *(Gossipy)* Like the things she told me about the couple at unit fourteen. You should *hear* what she says they get up to!

OLD LADY produces BINOCULARS then scans for scandals.

ROB

Just say you're a "friend" of mine, and the old girl would blab anything. From my whereabouts, work hours, recent guests, to the day I put out my washing.

Startled, ROB looks OFF.

ROB

Didn't I lose a t-shirt in my last wash?

ROB realises he's wearing the t-shirt.

ROB

Oh. No, I didn't.

Spotting something in BINOCULARS, OLD LADY totters OFF for a closer look.

LIGHTS OUT "ELSEWHERE".

ROB

What had I started?

ROB sits on COUCH. He points REMOTE at "TELEVISION" clicking channels in one hand, thumb-scrolling MOBILE in other, glancing between screens.

ROB

You hear of people like Adam. It's always in the news. Road-enraged short-fused nutjobs exploding into insane violence over trivialities. Everywhere online, waging tribal polarised wars, raging at each other from extreme perspectives. No middle ground for debate, excuse or calm discussion. This is my opinion, and this is my fist.

ROB leaps up and lifts "POWER DRILL".

SOUND FX: Power drill revs.

ROB

I fitted locks and stoppers to my windows.

ROB quickly drills at "WINDOW".

SOUND FX: Drilling.

ROB

I demanded a dead bolt from my landlord! He put it in. Then put up my rent.

ROB shrugs, then checks "FRONT DOOR" is secure.

ROB

Then I put in a spyhole.

ROB drills "SPY HOLE" in "FRONT DOOR".

SOUND FX: Drilling

ROB blows "SPY HOLE" clear, then spies out.

ROB

No one. *Yet.*

ROB drills another "SPY HOLE" at a different angle.

SOUND FX: Drilling

ROB peers out new "SPY HOLE".

ROB

All clear that way, too. *(Idea)* What if he ducks?

ROB kneels to drill "SPY HOLE" lower on "FRONT DOOR".

SOUND FX: Drilling

Still kneeling, ROB peers out.

ROB

Oh! Here comes my landlord.

Still on knees, ROB opens "FRONT DOOR" in greeting.

ROB

(Audience, dismayed) I had to pay for a new door.

Standing, ROB backs into room, casting nervous glances.

ROB

I couldn't live like this. There was only one
sensible course of action: Ring Adam and *demand*
he stop, once and for all or I'll call the police.
(Wavers) Do they still do witness protection?

ROB picks up MOBILE then stops.

ROB

Adam's number no longer existed on my phone.
None of them did. I'd been too thorough.

ROB scurries to DESK to search.

ROB

Had I written them? I scoured the house anyway.

ROB frantically searches around his "KITCHEN" then under the COUCH CUSHIONS. Nothing. He deflates.

ROB

What could I tell the police without evidence?
Without even Adam's full name.

ROB has an idea. He dials MOBILE.

ROB

My phone provider would log my incoming calls!

LIGHTS UP "ELSEWHERE".

Bored SUPPORT MINION with HEADSET looks up from COMIC, shakes head as though reading from a "SCREEN".

SUPPORT MINION

Nah, nothing on this number, mate.

ROB

(Phone) That's because I changed it. Check the
previous number?

SUPPORT MINION begrudgingly types on "KEYBOARD".

50

SUPPORT MINION

That number no longer exists on this account.

ROB

(Phone) But it's the same account. Surely there's still a call history.

SUPPORT MINION

You need to prove you're the account owner first. I'll send an authentication code.

SUPPORT MINION types at "KEYBOARD".

ROB impatiently looks at MOBILE.

ROB

(Phone) It hasn't come through.

SUPPORT MINION checks "SCREEN".

SUPPORT MINION

Says "Delivered" here.

ROB

(Phone) Which number did you send to?

SUPPORT MINION

The one the account was first registered with.

ROB

(Phone) But I changed that number.

SUPPORT MINION

Okay, I'll send another one.

SUPPORT MINION types at "KEYBOARD".

ROB

(Phone) Thank you.

ROB checks MOBILE. No message arrives.

ROB

(Phone) You've sent it to the old number again, haven't you.

SUPPORT MINION

I can only do what the system allows.

ROB

(Phone) Please. It's vital. *(Sob story)* I have to ring my Auntie. She's not long for this world. I've lost all her contact details and have no other way of finding them. Help me, Support Person 0B1-KN0B, you're my only hope.

SUPPORT MINION

(Doubtful) Not long for this world?

ROB

(Phone) Barely *days* left to live.

SUPPORT MINION

How'd you find that out?

ROB

(Phone) … Another auntie told me.

SUPPORT MINION

Get the number off her then?

ROB

(Phone) She told me by postcard on her mystery world cruise.
(Audience) My story sounded even dodgier when I said I didn't know where any of my relatives lived. Including my parents.

SUPPORT MINION

So, not one member of your family can give you this auntie's number?

ROB

(Phone) I'm adopted, and they all hate me. They're my phone records, let me have them!

SUPPORT MINION

We don't allow public access of that information.

ROB

(Phone) I thought you kept all our metadata these days?

SUPPORT MINION

That information is available only to Federal Police with a warrant, authorised government agencies, and marketing companies. We don't just hand it out willy-nilly. Not for free, anyway.

ROB

(Phone) But it's my data!

SUPPORT MINION

You should keep better track of it, then.

ROB

(Phone) So, you won't help me.

SUPPORT MINION

Not besides suggesting you make more effort to keep in touch with your family. They're your kin, man. Blood is thicker than water.

ROB

(Phone) Is this conversation being recorded for quality purposes?

SUPPORT MINION

Yeah.

ROB

(Audience) I suggested a place his company could archive it.

SUPPORT MINION mouths something unsavoury.

ROB

I was called something that might be considered an issue on later quality review.

LIGHTS DOWN "ELSEWHERE".

SUPPORT MINION departs.

ROB sits at DESK, types at "KEYBOARD".

ROB

I changed my number back, online. *(Peers at "SCREEN", relieved)* Luckily my old number was still available. Done! *(Presses decisively on "KEYBOARD")* I waited for Adam to call. *(Stares at MOBILE)* Nothing.

ROB places MOBILE face down on DESK.

ROB

A watched pot never boils.

ROB completely fails to relax.

ROB

I use a microwave.

ROB snatches up MOBILE. Disappointment – no calls have arrived.

An idea! ROB rushes out "FRONT DOOR" to other side of stage.

LIGHTS UP "ELSEWHERE".

SOUND FX: BAR NOISES

BARMAID enters "BAR", takes DISHCLOTH from divider BENCH and wipes it down.

ROB enters "BAR" from far side, looks round urgently.

ROB

I started visiting the pub where I first made the
fateful birthday card blunder. Just in case Adam
or Kate showed up again.

BARMAID notices ROB, continues wiping down "BAR".

ROB checks MOBILE, then looks around again.

ROB

If I could just talk to them face to face – without
getting mine smashed in. If I could even
remember Kate's face. For all I know, Adam had
mine stuck on a dartboard.

*ROB catches eyes with BARMAID, nods greeting. BARMAID nods
back, still polishing.*

ROB

What if I did find Kate – then Adam walked in
and saw us? And just attacked!

ROB dashes out of "BAR", then composes himself.

ROB

It was a chance I had to take.

ROB re-enters "BAR".

ROB

First, I visited on weeknights, in case it was a
regular haunt for after-work drinks.

ROB looks around, nods greeting at BARMAID who nods back.

ROB

Then I popped in on Friday nights.

ROB looks around, nods to BARMAID who gives friendlier nod back.

ROB

Then Saturdays.

ROB nods at BARMAID who nods with more enthusiasm.

ROB

And finally, Sunday sessions.

ROB nods at BARMAID. BARMAID gives coy wave back.

ROB

No sign of them. Obviously, Adam and Kate
weren't regulars here.

ROB notices BARMAID giving him a friendly smile, still polishing.

ROB

A barmaid began to recognise me, what with my
frequent visits.

An idea! ROB rushes over, grabs BAR MAT then searches for pen.

BARMAID offers PEN with enthusiasm. ROB scribbles on BAR MAT. BARMAID waits expectantly.

ROB

So, I gave her my phone number.

ROB hands BAR MAT to delighted BARMAID.

ROB

And told her to call if she saw any girl matching what I remembered of Kate's description.

BARMAID deflates, hopes dashed.

ROB

And *especially* if any big strong guys showed up.

BARMAID tosses BAR MAT, stalks OFF in frustration.

ROB

She seemed to serve other parts of the bar whenever I came in after that.

ROB walks out of "BAR".

ROB

So, I tried other bars in the area.

ROB circles to enter new "BAR" from a different angle.

BARMAID enters with DISHCLOTH polishing "glass".

ROB looks around the new "BAR".

ROB

Nope.

ROB rushes out, circles round to enter another new "BAR" from the far side of stage. BARMAID has walked across to swap bars too.

ROB looks around as BARMAID polishes "glass".

ROB

Nope.

ROB rushes out, circles round to enter "STRIP JOINT" from a different angle. BARMAID is doing a provocative dance with DISHCLOTH.

They stop and look at each other.

ROB

Is this even a bar?

BARMAID covers herself with DISHCLOTH, shakes head. ROB averts eyes, scampers out of "STRIP JOINT".

LIGHTS DOWN "ELSEWHERE".

BARMAID exits.

ROB

Did they even live near here? Would I have to search the entire city? It was impossible!

ROB enters through "FRONT DOOR", slumps on COUCH and sets MOBILE on COFFEE TABLE.

ROB

My friends said I looked ill. And I seemed to be going to the pub an *awful* lot. I couldn't explain, it sounded ridiculous even to me. But I had to find them. Before Adam found me and did whatever he did to … *(Can't recall)* That other guy.

A sound! ROB grabs nearby CRICKET BAT and scurries to "WINDOW".

ROB

I jumped at every sound in the night, ready to – or for – an attack.

No one outside. ROB tucks CRICKET BAT under arm as though dismissed and returns to COUCH, lying down.

LIGHTS LOW.

LIGHT EFFECT: ADAM's silhouette lurks.

ROB rolls fitfully on COUCH.

ROB

My sleep was filled with nightmares. Of dark

shadowy figures chasing me!

LIGHT EFFECT: ADAM's silhouette slowly walking.

ROB leaps up in fright – but can't move his legs!

ROB

My feet like lead! As though I were stuck in
quicksand. *(Forcing way along)* Like ploughing
through a snow drift, or a Franz Kafka novel.
Getting nowhere as the dark figure closes in.

LIGHTS UP in ROB's FLAT.

*ROB gasps as though suddenly woken. He looks behind but no one is
there.*

ROB pulls cheeks down as though looking in "MIRROR".

ROB

People at work noticed bags under my eyes.

ROB sticks out tongue, flinches at "reflection".

ROB

I felt unwell.

Feverish, ROB peels off PANTS, revealing BOXER SHORTS.

ROB

(Delirious) My stomach permanently churned. My

shoulders, heavy and laden, like a trapped dog, cowed and awaiting my fate.

ROB returns to COUCH, lays as though passed out.

LIGHTS low in ROB's FLAT.

SPOTLIGHT on ROB, flickering as though a TV is on.

ROB

One night, late, exhausted, I fell asleep to a late-night movie.

SOUND FX: Suspense thriller music – tense violins.

ROB

I was already living my own personal suspense thriller. I didn't need Hollywood's help.

ROB passes out asleep as …

Hooded FIGURE approaches "FRONT DOOR", knocks gruffly.

SOUND FX: Loud, assertive knocking.

FIGURE recedes to lurk near POWER BOX, back to audience.

Half-asleep, ROB sits up and checks non-existent watch.

ROB

Surely it was far too late for visitors.

ROB *blearily trudges to "FRONT DOOR" then suddenly freezes as he is about to open door.*

LIGHTS: *Flash/Freeze-frame effect*

ROB

The news was full of stories of people answering late-night callers who rush in and attack. What was I witlessly inviting?

In slow motion, ROB completes opening "FRONT DOOR" while also cringing in preparation for attack.

SOUND FX: *"Slow motion" Six Million Dollar Man sound effect*

LIGHTS UP *"ROB's FLAT".*

FIGURE *is revealed as a DRUNK BLOKE weeing against the wall.*

Finished, DRUNK BLOKE turns unsteadily, doing up his fly, possibly leaving what might be his penis out.

DRUNK BLOKE

Is this number twenty-three?

ROB *points at "FRONT DOOR".*

ROB

(Audience) He was too pissed to notice the number six on my door.

DRUNK BLOKE staggers back to take in the information.

DRUNK BLOKE
Number nine? I'm friggin' *miles* away!

ROB points "down the street" with entire arm.

ROB
(Audience) I gave him directions.

DRUNK BLOKE peers very closely along ROB's arm until reaching the pointing finger. Information received, DRUNK BLOKE salutes.

ROB
Ahem.

ROB points at DRUNK BLOKE's crotch. DRUNK BLOKE repacks and rezips, then points at ROB's boxers. ROB buttons his own fly. DRUNK BLOKE offers handshake. Mindful of what the hand has touched, ROB waves instead.

DRUNK BLOKE
Hope I didn't interrupt any sexy-sexy time going on in there. Ha! Eh? Eh?

DRUNK BLOKE gives obscene hand gesture, then stops and sniffs.

Leaning on ROB for balance, DRUNK BLOKE lifts his shoe and sniffs. It's bad but he continues OFF regardless.

ROB
As if I could think of sexy-sexy time while my

nemesis lurked out there and in every thought. As if I could sleep!

SOUND FX: Rob's MOBILE ring tone.

ROB closes "FRONT DOOR" and warily approaches MOBILE.

ROB
It was a totally unreasonable hour for anyone to be calling.

ROB picks up MOBILE and checks screen.

ROB
The number looked oddly familiar. Adam? Kate?

A deep breath, then ROB answers MOBILE.

SOUND FX: Muted nightclub music.

LIGHTS UP "ELSEWHERE".

JACINTA enters barefoot with MOBILE, dressed up but dishevelled – it's been quite a night. She holds SHOES in her other hand, trying to block her free ear.

JACINTA
(Sozzled, sing-songy) Pen-ny. It's me.

ROB
(Audience) Her tone changed when I said hello.

JACINTA stands abruptly upright, hand on hip.

JACINTA

You're not Penny. … Are you?

ROB

(Audience) Kate's friend! Bingo!
(Phone) No, but I *am* someone who needs to talk
to you.

JACINTA

Is this that creepy bloke from the pub? I told you
to piss off.

ROB

No, this is Rob.

JACINTA

Who?

ROB

The guy from Kate's birthday card.

JACINTA

Kate's birthday was ages ago.

ROB

I know.

JACINTA

So, what are you ringing me about it for?

ROB

I'm not.

JACINTA

Well, what the fuck, dude?

ROB

You rang me.

JACINTA

I pressed P for Penny. Put her on.

ROB

This isn't her number.

TAMMY staggers ON, barefoot, hair bedraggled over face.

TAMMY

(Sing-songy) Penn-ny!

TAMMY plonks herself unceremoniously on floor, as JACINTA checks MOBILE.

JACINTA

Ah, I pressed P for Prickface. Is that you?

ROB

Probably.

JACINTA

I need to organise my … thing. *(Tired)* I need a new phone. I need a lift!

ROB

Well, I'm not giving you one.

JACINTA

Dirty bastard.

ROB

A *lift*.

JACINTA

Shit no, you weirdo. Ringing me up like this, trying to crack on to me.

ROB

You rang me! It doesn't matter. I need to talk to Kate.

JACINTA

Kate isn't here!

TAMMY looks round then bellows OFF.

TAMMY

(Yelling) Kate!

JACINTA

(To TAMMY) Kate isn't here.
(Phone) Kate isn't here.

TAMMY

(Yelling) Kate!

JACINTA

(Phone) Are you deaf? Kate isn't here.

ROB

I don't mean right now. I just need her number.

JACINTA

You can't ring me to ask for some other girl's number!

TAMMY

F'ken cheek of it. *(Hiccups)*

JACINTA

(To TAMMY) It's some perve. Trying to score an easy root while I'm pissed.

TAMMY

Tell him to bugger off.

JACINTA

(Phone, impertinent) Hey. Hey! My mate says I should tell you to bugger off.

ROB

I will. As soon as you give me Kate's number. I'm not trying to pick up you, her, or anyone. There's just a big misunderstanding from her birthday that I need to sort out once and for all.

JACINTA

(Frowns) Kate's birthday was weeks ago.

ROB

I know!

TAMMY leans back and bellows OFF again.

TAMMY

(Yelling) Kate!

ROB

(Audience) I took a few deep calming breaths.

ROB breathes deeply, trying to find calm.

JACINTA

(Covers PHONE, to TAMMY) It's some heavy breather now.

TAMMY

Bloody weirdos!

ROB

(Phone) Please. I need Kate's number.

JACINTA

(Tired) Yeah, hang on.

JACINTA shuffles shoes and adjusts skirt then drops MOBILE.

ROB recoils from the deafening noise.

JACINTA

Shit. Fucking dropped it.

JACINTA struggles in tight dress to pick up MOBILE. TAMMY hiccups while nodding head to nightclub music beat. JACINTA opts to sit for a bit while she's down there.

JACINTA
Can you call us a taxi?

TAMMY
Taxi!

ROB
Sure, when you give me Kate's number.

TAMMY
I want to go clubbing. Where are my shoes?

ROB
Kate's number. Do you have it?

JACINTA
What? Yeah, sure. It's ... *(Stabs blearily at MOBILE)* Ah shit, I've taken a picture of myself.

TAMMY
Hey! Take one of my boobs.

Giggling, JACINTA and TAMMY make a laborious effort of a MOBILE photo down TAMMY's top.

ROB
(Phone) Hello? Hello?
(Audience) Could I just message her? Too risky. She was too sozzled to read it and would forget

71

by tomorrow. Or start all over in the morning with her hangover *and* temper to contend with? No thanks.
(Phone) Hello? Hello! Are you there?

JACINTA answers MOBILE curiously.

JACINTA

Hello?

ROB

Hello.

JACINTA

Who's this?

ROB

This is Rob.

JACINTA

Who's Rob?

TAMMY

Is he sexy? *(Giggles then hiccups)* Where are my shoes?

ROB

(Audience) Finally, blearily, I received the number.

JACINTA mouths digits – ROB dashes to DESK to write them.

ROB

(Audience) I asked her to repeat it, to make sure.

JACINTA

For fuck's sake. Oh-fucking-four. Two-fucking-two.

JACINTA mouths numbers and swear words as ROB checks.

ROB

(Audience) The numbers matched!
(Phone, sighs) What's your current location?

JACINTA

What do you want to know that for?

ROB

You wanted me to call you a taxi.

JACINTA

I'm perfectly fine. We're going to the nightclub.

TAMMY

Yay!

ROB

Have a great time.

JACINTA

Tell Penny to come down and join us.

ROB

Will do.

JACINTA staggers OFF, TAMMY crawls after her on all fours.

TAMMY

Where the frig are my shoes?

LIGHTS DOWN "ELSEWHERE".

ROB

(Audience) Mission accomplished. I had Kate's number.

ROB frowns at MOBILE.

ROB

And a blurry picture of someone's boobs. *(Determined)* One phone call tomorrow to finally sort this mess out. For the first time in a long time, I would sleep well and contented!

ROB departs to "BEDROOM", presses "LIGHT SWITCH".

LIGHTS DOWN ROB'S FLAT.

ROB departs OFF.

Silence for a beat.

SOUND FX: A bottle is broken in a street.

ROB rushes out, flicking "LIGHT SWITCH".

LIGHTS UP ROB'S FLAT

ROB *grabs* CRICKET BAT, *sits on* COUCH *ready for attack.*

LIGHTS DOWN SLOWLY *in* "ROB's FLAT"

SOUND FX: "PEER GYNT"

LIGHTS UP "ELSEWHERE".

SOUND FX: *A different mobile ringtone.*

KATE *enters, frowning at her* MOBILE, *then answers.*

KATE

Hello? ... Who?

LIGHTS UP *in* ROB'S FLAT

ROB *stands, talking on* MOBILE.

ROB

Rob. The guy who wrote on your birthday card.

KATE

My birthday was weeks ago.

ROB

I know.

KATE

How did you get my number?

ROB

I need to speak to your boyfriend, Adam.

KATE

You can't.

ROB

I have to!

KATE

He's not my boyfriend anymore.

ROB

Yes, he is. Isn't he?

KATE

We broke up. He's a cheating prick.

ROB

He was cheating?

KATE

Rub it in, why don't you. Why do you want him anyway?

ROB

Because he thought I was cheating with you.

KATE

I don't even know you.

ROB

I know. That's what I wanted to tell him.

KATE

That I cheat with guys I don't even know?

ROB

No! That it was totally stupid to think you're cheating with me.

KATE

I don't cheat at all.

ROB

Except for Simon.
(Audience, frowning) Or was that Scott? It was hard to keep track.

ROB listens at MOBILE as KATE recovers from shock.

ROB

(Audience) There was an iceberg of silence.

KATE

What do you know about Simon?

ROB

Nothing.

KATE

How did you find out about him and me then?

ROB

One of your friends told me. The point is, I need to speak to Adam.

KATE

It was Fiona, wasn't it. I knew that cow wouldn't keep a secret. Just because I got with Simon after she did.

ROB

Simon must be quite a guy.

KATE

I'm not speaking to him, ever since he got with Stacey.

ROB

Who's Stacey? *(Shakes head clear)* It doesn't matter. None of this stops you giving me his number.

KATE

Simon's?

ROB

No, Adam's!

KATE

I erased it. I don't want anything to do with that cheating prick again.

ROB

You have no contact details for him at all?

KATE

So, you can just go tell him about Simon? No frickin' way.

ROB

Look, I don't give a toss what you did with
Simon, or Scott, or Tom, Dick and Harry. I just
want Adam to stop hounding me like some
jealous psycho.

KATE

How do you know about Scott? Who the hell are
you?

ROB

I'm Rob.

KATE

Who? Hang on, you said Adam's jealous?

ROB

Either that or sociopathic. Both possibly.

KATE

Why? What has he done?

ROB begins to speak but falters.

ROB

(Audience) I drew a blank on actual proven cases
of … anything really. Saying it out loud to a
person, it seemed unreal. Deluded, even. Had
anything actually happened or was it all paranoia?
Seeing patterns that aren't there, like messages in
your tea-leaves or Jesus on your toast. Adam on
my doorstep. How much of fear is just looking
for things we think we see?

But then, I remembered the mouse head…

FX: "MOUSEHEAD ON DOORMAT" PICTURE ON BACK WALL

SOUND FX: OMINOUS BLARING CHORD

ROB

(Audience) I gave her a list of potential incidents.

KATE

And you're sure it's Adam doing this? Out of blind jealous rage over me?

ROB

(Phone) He sounds half demented each time he calls about you.

KATE

(Disappointed) Only half demented?

ROB

(Shrugs) Totally demented at times.

KATE

So, he does still care for me!

ROB

Eh?

KATE

He didn't seem to even care when I dumped him. But if he's actually livid with anger and jealousy.

ROB

Actually, his last call *was* quite a while ago.

KATE

I mean, he's always *talked* about punching walls and smashing windows and stuff. And he's decked quite a few guys who tried it on with me. And the whole Scott thing of course.

ROB

(Pleading) What did he do to Scott?

KATE

But I always thought that was all talk. Besides the actual punching walls, smashing windows and decking people. And the restraining orders. And that whole court thing. But you're saying he did all this for me? *(Decisive)* I'm going to call him.

ROB

You don't have his number.

KATE

I'll get it off Kevin.

ROB

Who's Kevin?

KATE

Don't you know Kevin?

ROB

I don't know anyone! Technically, I don't even

know you.

KATE

A shame, really. I thought something was starting
to happen.

ROB

With me?

KATE

No, with Kev. Fuck, he's fit.

ROB

But *I* need to talk to Adam. Seriously!

KATE

So do I. Thank you so much, Ron.

ROB

Rob.

KATE

Probably the whole reason he cheated was
because he thought you keep trying to root me.

ROB

But I haven't!

KATE

And you never will, Ron. I'm really sorry, I know
how much that must crush you.

ROB

But it doesn't.

KATE

I'm going to tell him everything you just said.

ROB

No! Don't!

KATE

Every detail. Thank you, Ron. You may have just prevented Adam and I from making the biggest, most horrible mistake of our lives.

KATE hangs up and rushes OFF.

LIGHTS DOWN "ELSEWHERE".

ROB stares aghast at MOBILE.

ROB

By making the biggest, most horrible mistake of mine.

LIGHTS DOWN ROB'S FLAT.

SOUND FX: Clock ticking.

LIGHTS UP slowly on ROB'S FLAT.

ROB is hunched on COUCH, clutching nearby CRICKET BAT,

MOBILE on COFFEE TABLE.

SOUND FX: Tin can kicked along a street.

ROB leaps up to "WINDOW", peers out with paranoid eyes. No one. He checks "FRONT DOOR" is locked.

ROB

Times like these you realise how tenuous your safety is. The news bulletins are right. Nowhere is safe. Our homes must be fortresses. No wonder the lady next door bought herself a watchdog.

LIGHTS UP "ELSEWHERE".

OLD LADY neighbour backs ON, tugging LEASH.

SOUND FX: Large dog growling noises.

OLD LADY is violently yanked OFF by LEASH.

LIGHTS DOWN "ELSEWHERE".

ROB

How have we come to this? How had I?

SOUND FX: Rob's MOBILE ring tone.

LIGHTS UP "ELSEWHERE"

ADAM stands menacingly, waiting on his MOBILE.

ROB *warily answers MOBILE.*

ADAM

Is that someone called Rod?

ROB

(Phone, automatically correcting) Rob.

ROB *realises what he has done, aghast.*

ROB

(Audience) Oh god. Perhaps the only reason Adam hadn't found me was the difference of a single letter. I was a dead man.

ADAM

You. Are. A. *Champion.*

A beat as ROB *tries to process this information.*

ROB

(Audience) "It's a trap!" was my only thought. I remained silent.

ADAM

Mate, I dunno what you said to Kate, but it worked a bloody treat.

ROB

(Audience) I gave a non-committal "Oh."
(Phone) Oh.

ADAM

We're back together again. Better than ever.

ROB

… Oh.

ADAM

And today, I popped the question. And mate –
she said yes.

ROB

(Audience) I offered what I hoped sounded like
hearty congratulations. Adam gushed with details.
Had he rung the wrong person?

*ADAM mouths excited talk, with a couple of gynaecological gestures,
explaining how well things are going.*

ROB

(Audience) Somehow, I'd forced them to come to
their senses, realise the depths of their passions.
They were now completely in love. *Proper* love.

ADAM

Not just rooting. And all that other shit like
buying a house and having kids, too.

ROB

(Phone, relieved) Well, at least this means you can
probably stop stalking after me at last.

Silence. ROB's face falls.

ADAM

I've been doing *what?*

ROB

(Audience) I stammered through my list of terrors. Some real, most very probably imagined. Adam went quiet. I awaited my fate.

ADAM

(Laughs) Nah, not me, mate. Barely knew you from a bar of soap before today.

ROB

(Phone) But, what about ... *(Waves hand, sees nothing)* All the things.

ADAM

What things?

ROB

The mouse?

ADAM

I don't even know how to use a computer.

ROB

(Audience) And then I realised: *I* was the short-fused nutjob exploding into insane acts after leaping to conclusions. *I* was the one reading into nothings, skimming details, joining dots without following the numbers.

ADAM

Gotta say, sounds a bit bloody paranoid to me, mate. *(Deduces)* You're a single fella, aren't you?

ROB

(Audience) I admitted so, but insisted it absolutely was *not* a factor in all this.

ADAM

Been single for a while, too? Think it's just for pissing out of?

ROB

(Phone) Who has time for that when… *(Waves round weakly)* All the things.

ADAM

What you need is a nice girlie. Soon set you right.

ROB

(Audience) I struggled for a reply.

ROB *can't think of what to say. Bows head.*

ROB

(Phone) … Maybe.

ADAM

Tell you what. I'll pass your number to a smick piece I know. Friend of a mate's ex. She's having a bit of a dry stretch herself.

ROB

(Phone) That totally isn't necessary.
(Audience) He didn't take no for an answer, much less even notice it.

ADAM

Dip your wick, mate.

ADAM hangs up, turns to leave but stops. He checks the underside of his shoe – it smells.

With a frown, ADAM wipes shoe on ground, then departs OFF.

ROB moves down centre.

ROB

(Audience) True to his word, Adam passed my number on to this female friend of a mate's ex.

SOUND FX: ROB'S MOBILE rings.

ROB looks at MOBILE.

ROB

I didn't recognise the number. I usually let unknown numbers through to voicemail. You know – telemarketers.

ROB answers.

LIGHTS UP "ELSEWHERE".

FRIEND OF A MATE'S EX enters, on MOBILE call.

FRIEND OF A MATE'S EX

Hello. Is that someone called … Rob?

ROB

(Phone) Yes. Yes, it is.
(Audience) So we talked…

They lower MOBILES as FRIEND OF A MATE'S EX approaches to stand face to face with ROB.

ROB

And then we met.

They smile at each other.

ROB

And we got along. Really well.

FRIEND OF A MATE'S EX notices ROB's boxers. ROB quickly buttons up.

ROB

She encouraged me to get out a bit more. Get some fresh air.

FRIEND OF A MATE'S EX motions for ROB to venture out. He warily steps out of his flat, blinks in the sunlight of a beautiful day.

ROB

Come on out. The water's fine.

FRIEND OF A MATE'S EX leans in to whisper in ROB's ear.

ROB

She also suggested some *much* better indoor
activities than sitting in wait for psychos to attack.

Smiles. They turn forward, hand in hand.

ROB

We're seeing each other. And you know what?

FRIEND OF A MATE'S EX

It's going great. Really great.

They smile at her finishing his sentence.

ROB

And we both agreed wholeheartedly *never* to go
near Adam, Kate or any of their friends again.

*With a coy nod, FRIEND OF A MATE'S EX leads ROB towards
"BEDROOM" but they stop short.*

ROB

(*Audience*) Oh. Apparently, Adam and Kate sent
us a wedding invite. Christ only knows who that
ended up with.

They depart OFF to "BEDROOM".

END

Principle Props

- BENCH/COUNTER dividing stage
- COUCH with CUSHIONS
- COFFEE TABLE
- DESK with CHAIR
- PEN and PAPER.
- multiple MOBILE PHONES
- DOOR MAT
- remains of a wrapped KEBAB (ROB's pocket)
- TEA TOWELS/DISHCLOTHS
- SPATULA
- BICYCLE HELMET
- MAGAZINE on coffee table
- TIE and JACKET
- TOOTHBRUSH
- HI-VIS VEST, HARDHAT, and CLIPBOARD
- LETTERS/MAIL
- Telephone HEADSET
- OPENED LETTER on coffee table
- BINOCULARS

- MAGAZINE/COMIC
- BAR MAT and PEN
- CRICKET BAT
- silky BOXER SHORTS
- long DOG LEASH

About the Author

Martin Lindsay is a Western Australian writer hidden away in the leafy seaside town of Dunsborough.

He is the author of the plays *Spd D8n*, *One Night One Day* and *Brown Acid*, and award-winning one-act plays *One Night Stand Off* and *Past Loves*.

Other plays include one-act *Someone Called Rob*, and finalists in the Short + Sweet and Arkfest ten-minute play festivals with *Couch*, *The Retirement Gift*, *That Little Voice*, and *Possum Play*.

Martin was a contributing writer for *Lifted* in the 2013 Perth Fringe Festival, and co-wrote and directed the comedy monologue/burlesque *Lock-In Love* for the 2014 Adelaide Fringe Festival and 2014 Melbourne Comedy Festival.

Martin's short stories have been included in Black Inc's *Best Australian Stories 2012*, and won the 2013 Stringybark Humorous Short Story Competition, the 2014 Joe O'Sullivan Writers Prize, and the 2019 Peter Cowan Short Story award. His micro-fiction has appeared in Short and Twisted editions and Night Parrot Press' *Once* (2020), *Twice Not Shy* (2021), and *Three Can Keep a Secret* (2022) collections.

He is even known to occasionally blog on his website at martinlindsay.net, when not trying to stop parrots from having sex on his balcony railing.

Martin's debut novel *Wil, Maree and the Mattress* will be available soon from Moody Lapcat Books.

Plays by the Same Author

- Spd D8n

- One Night One Day

- Brown Acid

- Past Loves

- Couch

- Framed

- The Retirement Gift

- That Little Voice

- Possum Play

- Third Date's the Charm

Spd D8n

A play in two acts by
Martin Lindsay

Spd D8n

A play in two acts by
Martin Lindsay

At a speed dating evening at a local pub, five singles consider the question – How much can you really learn about someone in four minutes?

Ahead of them is a night of hope, hell, and free Cosmopolitans.

And maybe the chance to find what they didn't know they were looking for.

*"Hang on. I'm not **quite** drunk enough to make it to the end of your story."*

"How did you get into that line of work? Did you not study or something?"

"That possibly came across as a bit needy."

"Polyamory sounds an awful lot like just rootin' around."

"They call me Mike. Rhymes with bike. Maybe you can ride me sometime."

Available now from Moody Lapcat Books.

Past Loves

A play in one act by
Martin Lindsay

Ben is having a very good year. It just doesn't happen to be the current one.

Invited to coffee by his best mate's wife, Ben's life ... lives ... are about to be turned upside down.

And not just by the price of a latte these days.

'It happened before I could stop it. If I'd only known where things would go ...'

'Where did things go?'

'Where do you think things went!'

'I've heard a lot about you, Ben.'

'This will work much better with open minds.'

'If not completely vacant ones.'

Available now from Moody Lapcat Books.

One Night One Day

**A play in two acts by
Martin Lindsay**

A comedy about singles
and social graces, after
a night that went so
right goes so wrong the
next morning.

Rachel and Greg wake up together after a night out on the
town, much to the surprise of both.

An awkward situation at the best of times, made all the more
awkward as details from the previous night slowly filter back
to them…

Coming soon from Moody Lapcat Books.

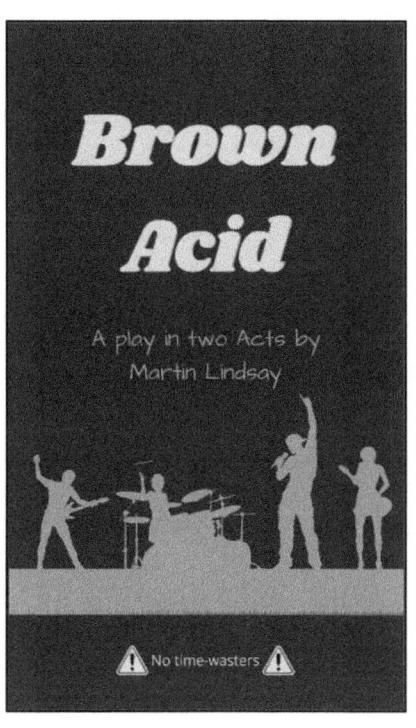

Brown Acid

A play in two acts by
Martin Lindsay

Throughout rock'n'roll
history, from small
beginnings sometimes
legendary bands grow...

And sometimes, they
don't.

Wanted:

Musicians to join original four-piece rock band.

Serious gigging opportunities with a group that is going
places. Own transport would suit.

NO TIME WASTERS!

Coming soon from Moody Lapcat Books.

Moody Lapcat Books

Books better than belly rubs

Moody Lapcat Books is an independent publisher of books and plays.

Visit moodylapcatbooks.com to see our latest releases, things to come, or enquire about performance rights.

Or contact@moodylapcatbooks.com

www.ingramcontent.com/pod-product-compliance
Lightning Source LLC
Chambersburg PA
CBHW070329120726
47909CB00008B/2657